The MOUSE and the MOOSE

ROBERT SCHMiDT

Illustrated by: Salvador Capuyan

ISBN: Softcover   978-1-5144-7150-0
        EBook   978-1-5144-7149-4

Print information available on the last page

Rev. date: 03/02/2016

To order additional copies of this book, contact:
Xlibris
1-888-795-4274
www.Xlibris.com
Orders@Xlibris.com

Dedicated to Peter Marimen

In a Forest near the town
that is simply known as "Trenz"
is where we start our story
of two quite different friends

WELCOME
TO
TRENZ

There were birds and bees and butterflies
And flowers in a row
And trees that seemed to touch the sky
And rivers steady flow

Of all the creatures in the woods
The largest one of all
Was the wise old Moose named "Noah"
He stood near ten feet tall

But Noah because he was quite old
No longer young and spree
His eyesight now was failing him
Poor Noah could barely see

And also in this forest
Lived creatures mild and meek
But none was any smaller
Than a field mouse known as "Squeak"

4

Squeak was very timid
And always getting hurt
Because he was the smallest mouse
He learned to stay alert

Then one bright and sunny day
While Squeak was digging holes
The ground began to shake and roll
Beneath his quivering toes

Squeak held on and closed his eyes
His face grew white and pale
And when the ground was finally still
He could not move his tail

He opened up his eyes to see
Just what had pinned him down
Was Noah's big and furry hoof
At least ten inches round!

So Squeak called out in terror
As his voice began to fail
"Could you please remove your foot kind sir?"
"It's resting on my tail."

As Noah realized what he'd done
He quickly moved his foot
"Excuse me sir" He answered back
"I thought it was a root"

"You see" he said as he bent his head
Much closer to the lawn
"I simply did not see you"
"My eyesight's almost gone"

10

So Squeak gazed up, no longer scared
And asked his new found friend
"How do you eat?" Squeak quickly said
His nerve's now on the mend.

"It's very hard to find the food.
This is the hardest feat
I spend almost all of my time
Just finding food to eat."

"If only I could see again
The apples on the trees
I'd eat until my tummy's full
As many as I please."

"Well maybe I could help you"
Squeak bravely volunteered

"I'll sit perched high upon your crown
Or cuddled in your beard"

13

"And when we've eaten all the fruit
Each apple, pear, and peach
I'll shimmy up the highest limbs
For fruits you cannot reach"

"And even if we eat them all
The fruit gone from the trees
We'll simply swim across the pond
As often as we please"

Noah paused and thought a bit
Then finally spoke these words.
"You'll sit atop my antlers
And fly among the birds."

17

"I'll keep you high up off the ground
And out of dangers way
Keep you warm on chilly nights
And dry on rainy days"

"From this day on" as Noah exclaimed
"We'll always have each other."
"I'll care for you, you'll care for me
As if we both were brothers."

And that indeed is what took place
In the woods outside of Trenz
The Mouse and the Moose lived
evermore
From that day as best friends

About the author

He is a grandfather of 7 who was inspired by his own grandfather,
who had to quit school in the eighth grade when his father died,
so he could help support his family. He never stopped learning and
loved to write rhythmical poetry. This book is dedicated to him.

Edwards Brothers Malloy
Oxnard, CA USA
March 18, 2016